Cici:

A Dog's Tale

Cici:
A Dog's Tale
by
Nicola Hedges

Published by Blue Poppy Publishing.

Cover art and illustrations by Rebecca Beesley.

ISBN: 978-1-911438-13-7

To Karen and Lexi.

Note: For anyone who is unsure; Cici is pronounced 'see-see'

Chapter One
Abandoned

It was a very cold winter's day when she was taken away. There were no goodbyes. She had to go. It was as simple as that.

When the time came, her master marched her out of the house. Without a word, he jerked her to get into the back of his car. Then he drove off in complete silence. At first, she recognised sounds and smells from the park, the café, and the butcher. He drove further and faster. Buildings and trees flashed past and then gave way to open countryside, fields and woods. It was hard to tell where they were going. Nothing was familiar now. His mood was ugly. She sensed it and it made her feel very afraid.

Eventually, he stopped by a deserted track which was bordered on both sides by a dense line of trees, the branches of which were laden with snow. As he opened the car door, she lowered her body onto the seat as if trying to root herself to the spot with her nails digging into the seat cover. However, her master was big and strong and was easily able to dislodge her and scoop her up in his muscular arms and set her down outside the car onto the freezing snow. He removed her collar and lead impatiently. She tried to scramble back inside the car, her paws slipping and sliding on the cold metal, but he blocked the entrance with his arm, pushed her out of the way and quickly slammed the door. Angrily, he got back into the driver's seat and drove off without a word. She tried to run after him, but he was driving too fast.

Alone and cold, Cici stood for what seemed like forever. Her beautiful hazel eyes roved with fear and uncertainty, desperately trying to work out where she was. Her nostrils twitched and flared as she sniffed the air to see if she could detect any familiar scents, but there were none. She wanted her master to come back for her, to take her home with him, but she sensed he would not.

What was she to do? She did not know the way home. Also, she knew it was a long way off. She knew she would not be welcome even if she could get back. The cold crept up through her paws. She knew instinctively that she must move. Unsure of where she was heading, she began to walk slowly along the virgin snow with her head bowed, stepping into her new life.

The snowfall was heavy that day and as the snowflakes fell from the sky and landed on her smooth, chestnut coat, she shivered and then shook as she tried to get them off. She was fighting a losing battle though.

As she walked, she felt the snow being compressed beneath each paw making a soft, crunching sound. It served as a distraction for a while until the biting pain of the cold brought her back to the present. The hours rolled by and night came. Cici needed to find shelter. In the near distance, she saw a wild, wiry looking silhouette against the backdrop of the moonlit sky. Her hackles went up. She edged closer and studied it with her head tilted trying to work out what it was. Gradually, she relaxed a little as she found that the shape was a mass of tangled branches with a well trampled entrance leading to a den inside. It was ideal. As she went in, the twigs which littered the floor, brittle with the cold, snapped beneath her young paws. She circled around the space a few times and then dropped her tired, hungry body down and curled herself up tightly with her cold, wet, black nose placed firmly under her bushy tail. However, sleep did not come as she listened instinctively.

She heard something outside which made her heart race. She could tell that it was nearby. She was scared it would pick up her scent and come for her. It moved slowly and carefully through the snow. Occasionally, it stopped and snuffled at the ground, perhaps in search of something to eat and then it would jump. She could see the creature's shape in the moonlight. It had what appeared to be spiky tipped branches on its head at one end and a stumpy tail at the other. For a moment, it stopped in its tracks and looked in her direction. She stayed as still as she could, holding her breath, bracing herself for what might follow, but then all of a sudden it leapt in the air and bounded away, disappearing from view. She let out a long, quiet sigh of relief.

As she gazed into the night she saw flurries of snowflakes illuminated by the moon, falling gracefully from the sky. It reminded her of her first winter when she chased and pounced happily, snuffling and snorting through the deeper drifts, but that was in another lifetime.

Soon she found herself thinking about her family. She had been with them since she was a pup. They all thought she was so cute and loved her back then. The young girl used to play with her all the time. They enjoyed lots of cuddles and walks together and were such good friends. Cici was so happy.

However, as she got bigger, they seemed to lose interest in her. Sometime later, the master of the family started to become bossy and impatient. He would bark commands at Cici, most of which she did not understand. She knew when she had misunderstood them though because he would push her out of the way impatiently. He had a loud, booming voice and used it way too much. He would shout out about something called 'money' a lot. He always seemed so angry whenever anyone mentioned the word. It upset and scared her so much that, whenever he started, she used to hide under the kitchen table with her soft, floppy ears lying flat against her head, trying to block out the sound of his voice. Her brow was always furrowed as she felt really nervous. After the shouting came the mistress's tears. There were so many of them and so often. Cici would go and sit with her. Her heart felt like lead. The mistress would occasionally stroke Cici, talking gently to her in between sobs but on other occasions, she would just cry herself to sleep. Cici would lie faithfully by her side, feeling her sadness with all her being.

Feelings of isolation and emptiness welled up inside her as she reminisced. If she were able to cry, she would have sobbed her heart out then and there. She just could not understand why she had been abandoned and she wondered what was to become of her now.

Her thoughts were interrupted by the sound of dogs barking somewhere in the distance and then there was silence again. Gradually, the darkness enveloped Cici and she fell into a deep sleep. Her cold body juddered and twitched as flashbacks of her life appeared in her dreams. She whimpered quietly now and then but nobody heard her.

The following morning, Cici reluctantly opened her eyes. The den was flooded with a bright, bluish light as the sun sparkled through the thin wall of frozen snowflakes which covered the entrance. She stared at it for a while, fascinated. Then she got up and started pawing at it. When the hole was big enough, she poked her head out. The coldness of the air hit her. She yawned, stretched and boldly stepped into the thick, carpet of snow. Her paws sunk deep and wearily she trudged on again.

She really was beginning to tire when she picked up the scent of other dogs. Just ahead of her, she saw a tree with long, hanging branches. Cautiously, she approached. She saw a litter of four black pups. They were all huddled together. She felt a slight sense of relief to see her own kind again and looked forward to meeting them. She edged nearer. She thought they were sleeping at first but as she got closer, they all raised their heads and stared at her. Then, all of a sudden, from behind the tree trunk, their mother emerged, head lowered and growling. Cici froze. The dog's hackles were up as she moved forward menacingly. She looked so fierce with her narrowed, wild eyes and white, sharp teeth bared. The warning was loud and clear. Cici turned and ran away as fast as she could with her tail between her legs. She ran and ran until she was out of breath. She glanced around and was very relieved to see that the dog was nowhere in sight. Feeling hurt and rejected, she continued on her way, alone again.

Chapter Two
At The Farm

By the afternoon, she arrived at a place where the track and the trees came to an abrupt end. Beyond that point, the land stretched out in front of her like a great, white, bumpy quilt. She stood there and sniffed, trying to catch the scent of something, anything that would lead her to a source of food as her stomach, which was empty, rumbled and groaned. Then she smelt something which reminded her of home – wood smoke. She followed the scent across a couple of fields and down a hill to a small cluster of farm buildings. As she drew closer, she could see smoke billowing out of a chimney on a cottage. She sat and rested, watching the farm. It was not long before a door opened and out came a small, black dog followed by a woman wearing a long skirt covered by an apron. Her head hidden in a thick scarf. They walked briskly across the yard and disappeared inside a huge barn. Cici wondered if the dog would be aggressive like the last one. There was a lot of banging and clattering in the barn and then the woman's voice drifted up to Cici as she called quietly and encouragingly to whatever animals were in the barn. The dog trotted out and around the yard sniffing about and disappearing in between machinery and piles of stuff hidden beneath the snow. At the top of a small mound the dog stopped, turned and seemed to look straight at Cici. She lowered her body close to the ground, trying to make herself invisible. Silently, she waited. There was no barking or growling. The dog simply wagged its tail and trotted back to the cottage and waited for the woman as she struggled to carry a heavy bucket. Then they both scuttled indoors out of the cold.

Cici waited a while before moving stealthily towards the cottage, hiding behind a low wall. She was unsure what to do having made it there but, before she could decide, she heard scratching coming from behind the front door. Intrigued, she went over to investigate. Ears pricked up and head moving from side to side, she listened carefully. Along with the scratching, she could hear a quiet whining noise. Then, footsteps on a wooden floor inside, heading towards the door and the woman's voice asking the dog, whom she called Lilly, what was wrong in a really kind and friendly way. The dog scratched and whined more urgently. The door handle turned and through the slight gap, Cici saw the dog's muzzle as it opened the door impatiently. Lilly rushed outside. She circled Cici a number of times and then started sniffing her excitedly. Cici stayed still. She was so relieved that this dog was friendly. She looked up at the woman with sad, yearning eyes. The woman bent down and gently stroked the top of Cici's head, talking to her in calm, reassuring way then gestured for her to go inside. The woman reminded Cici of her mistress back home but she hesitated at the doorway, worried that there might be a master inside. When Lilly trotted past her quite happily, she followed her in. The room, although quite small and bare, was lovely and warm. Cici crept past the fireplace and hid under a chair.

The woman disappeared into the kitchen and returned with a bowl of chicken stew in each hand. She placed them on the floor, one out in front of Cici and one in front of Lilly. Slowly, Cici emerged from under the chair. In no time at all, they had both gulped the lot down. With her stomach feeling less empty, she curled up on the rug near Lilly in front of the glowing fire. It didn't take Cici long to fall into a deep sleep. The woman sat knitting in her comfortable but well-worn armchair and when she was ready for bed she bid her two companions goodnight before heading upstairs.

During the night, Cici was very restless and whimpered a lot. She was having nightmares. Lilly woke up several times, disturbed by the noises she made. Each time, she looked at Cici to make sure that she was okay. At one point the woman must have heard Cici too because she came back downstairs and sat with her for a while.

The following morning, Cici woke to the delicious smell of sausages. She followed the smell into the kitchen where the woman was cooking her breakfast. When she saw Cici, she filled a bowl with more of the stew and placed it on the floor for her. Cici eagerly ate it all. Lilly was lying under one of the chairs. She looked very contented. Cici thought she must have already eaten her breakfast as there was an empty bowl beside hers. When Cici had finished, she curled up under a chair as well. The woman carried on cooking and when she had finished, she sat down at the table and began to eat her breakfast with one dog on the floor either side of her. When the woman's plate was almost empty, she stopped and then gave each dog half a sausage, much to their delight.

After breakfast, the woman let both dogs out of the house and went about her daily work on the farm. The dogs then went their separate ways. Lilly disappeared round the back of one of the buildings while Cici went over to one of the larger buildings. She saw that the big, wooden door was slightly ajar. She walked over to the door and stopped. She sniffed the air. There were lots of different smells drifting out of the building. As she got closer to the entrance she stuck her head through the opening. She could hear a steady murmuring. Excited by what she might find, she went inside and was amazed by what she saw. She had never seen so many hens in one place at the same time. There was a fence surrounding them. She stood next to it and watched them through the narrow bars for a bit, studying them. Some were milling around scratching and pecking at the ground while others were lined up along the feeding stations eating the food inside. Cici was mesmerised as she watched their heads bobbing up and down. In one corner some of the hens were fighting, pecking at each other and flapping their wings wildly. The rest seemed to be just resting.

Her attention was drawn to a smell. It was very familiar and it was lovely. It was something that she used to eat when she was back home sometimes. She scanned the enclosure. She could not see where it was coming from. A thin line of saliva dripped from her mouth. She paced up and down in front of the fence impatiently, trying to figure out how she would be able to get over it. She saw a bale of hay at one end. She clambered onto it and, without hesitation, leapt over the fence and landed among the startled hens.

The hens flapped and fluttered and ran squawking in all directions. Cici was so intent on finding the source of the smell that she ignored the din and ran around excitedly with her nose to the ground. Among some straw she found them – eggs. The hens sitting on them began to peck at her and squawked frantically. Their beaks hurt her nose and she backed off. She trotted in another direction. Hens were rushing at her from all angles. Cici felt the draught of their flapping wings. Finally, her nose led her to a spot where there were some broken eggs. She lapped them up with great enthusiasm. As she was polishing off the remainder of the eggs, she was suddenly aware that there were even more hens around her. They rushed at her, beating their wings furiously. One fluttered onto her back and one was on her head. She was backed into a corner. Their beaks felt as if they were drilling into her body. They were angry. She was scared. She needed to get out. She barked. She bared her teeth and growled and then she rushed at them but could make no headway. They closed in again. The volume of their noise was deafening. Their pecks forced Cici to perform a kind of 'dance' as she thrashed her body from side to side trying unsuccessfully to get out of their way. She was trapped and terrified. She used all her strength to scramble up the fence, but it was too high. She tried again and again but on each attempt she failed.

Just when Cici thought all hope had gone and was resigned to her fate, the door of the building flew open and in ran the woman, armed with a stick, and Lilly by her side. Having heard the noise coming from the building and seeing that the door was open, she thought the hens were being attacked by a feral animal. As they went inside, they saw that Cici was being attacked. She looked so helpless and was yelping. Lilly barked loudly trying to warn the hens off her while the woman opened the gate on the fence and went inside. She closed it quickly behind her and waded through the sea of hens and used her stick to direct them out of her path until she reached Cici. Then she bent down, lifted her up in her arms and carried her to safety, shutting the gate firmly behind her.

With the egg raider gone, the hens soon settled down. Cici, however, was still in shock and trembled like a leaf. She slunk out of the building, battered and defeated. She stopped and licked her smarting wounds for a while, trying to ease the pain. Eventually she plodded back to the cottage where she sat and waited patiently until the woman came and opened the door. She checked Cici over to make sure she had not been seriously hurt and fussed over her for a bit before she went back outside to carry on with her daily chores. Cici curled up on the rug in front of the fire where she quickly fell asleep, still trembling. She remained there for most of the day. It was a disturbed sleep though as she tossed and turned making lots of yelping and growling noises.

Later that evening, the woman called to Lilly and Cici to have their evening meal in the kitchen. While Lilly rushed to get hers, Cici did not. Although she had heard the woman, she felt unable to move. Seeing that Cici had not come when she called, the woman brought the bowl of food to her instead. She gently encouraged her to eat. Wanting to please the woman, Cici slowly licked at the food until it had all gone.

The woman went to bed early that night but before she went upstairs she checked on Cici. She did not seem right. The woman was worried about leaving her downstairs so she lifted her up and carried her up to her room. She placed her gently onto her bed and snuggled up to her, trying to comfort her. Cici felt the reassuring warmth radiating from the woman's body and fell into a deep, undisturbed sleep.

The next morning, Cici was the first to wake. She felt better and wanted to share that with the woman. She lifted her paw and placed it on the woman's shoulder. Nothing happened. She did it again but this time she made a whining noise at the same time. The woman slowly opened her eyes. The first thing she saw was Cici's face as it hovered close to hers. Cici had a funny expression on her face as her mouth was slightly open with only her lower front teeth showing and she was making a gruff 'err' sound. The woman smiled. She was relieved that Cici was in a playful mood so she sat up and invited her to play. Cici gently mouthed her hands and pounced, wriggled and rolled on the bed until the woman was ready to get up.

After breakfast, they all went outside together. This time though, Cici never left the woman's side except for when she went into the larger building to feed the hens and to collect the eggs they had laid. She had learned her lesson. Otherwise, she enjoyed following the woman and Lilly around the farm. It felt good to be in their company and she found it interesting as she got to see things she had not seen before, like cows being milked and meeting sheep for the first time.

After the woman had finished her work for the day, she returned home with the dogs in tow. She fed them the last of the chicken stew before cooking her own meal and settling down in her armchair to knit. The dogs were curled up comfortably on the rug in front of the fire. Every now and then, Cici looked up at the woman and gazed at her. Several hours passed and the woman went upstairs to bed while the dogs remained on the rug downstairs. Very soon, they were all asleep.

Just past midnight, as Cici was in the middle of a dream where she was playfully chasing the little girl around the garden on a beautiful, hot, sunny day, she heard something which did not fit the scene. A handle turned. A hinge squeaked. She felt a blast of cold air. She opened her eyes. Footsteps creaked on a wooden floor. She saw the shape of a man in the darkness. Lilly was as still as a statue on the rug beside her, sitting to attention. Cici stayed put and did not make a sound. The man stopped at the foot of the stairs. He looked around and caught sight of the shape of the two dogs against the dim glow of the fire. He started towards them but then shook his head, turned abruptly muttering under his breath and stumbled upstairs. Although Lilly curled up on the rug again, Cici felt on edge and did not sleep much as the darkness dragged on and on.

The next morning, the sound of voices drifted down the stairs. The man's voice was getting louder and louder. 'Money' and 'can't afford' were mentioned. The woman became more and more upset. The conversation ended abruptly. A door slammed shut. Heavy feet stomped down the stairs. Lilly went and hid behind the armchair. Cici stayed on the rug, head bowed, ears flat against her head, waiting. It was as if she knew what was coming next. The man marched over to her, picked her up roughly and carried her outside the cottage. He set her down on the ground and pointed into the distance, shouting something at her. He went back inside and slammed the door angrily behind him. There was no mistaking his orders.

Cici stood there stunned. She could not believe it. Just when she thought she had found a loving family where she felt she could belong, he had wrecked everything. She howled as loudly as she could at the injustice of it all. She looked up at the window one last time. She saw the woman staring back at her, tears cascading down her cheeks. Cici did not want to leave. Not like this. Suddenly, the door swung open. The man appeared, brandishing a stick. Fearing for her life, she fled. She shot past the farm buildings, across several fields and up a hill until she could run no more. Panting heavily, she turned around and looked down at the cluster of farm buildings for one last time. Feeling distraught and not caring where she was going, she followed a path along the ridge in a complete daze.

Chapter Three
The Traveller

The snow had already begun to melt and, as the day went on, the warmth of the sun started to reveal patches of the once hidden landscape beneath.

Cici wandered across the fields, most of which had become sodden and slushy. As she walked, partially melted snow mixed with mud spattered upwards onto her cold, tired body. She crawled under and jumped over fences, slid down ditches and clambered up slippery banks as she passed through one field to the next. At the edge of one of the fields was a barbed wire fence with wooden posts. When Cici crawled beneath it, a barb caught one of her hind legs and, as she tried to free herself, it ripped a piece of her skin. She let out an ear-piercing yelp and, even though she was in a lot of pain, she carried on wriggling until she reached the other side of the fence. As blood seeped from her wound, it became mixed with the mud on her coat making it almost indistinguishable. She limped onwards and stopped only occasionally to lick her wound. After a while, numbed by the cold, the pain subsided.

By the time it was dark, Cici felt exhausted. She had to stop and rest at some point but did not know when or where, so she just carried on aimlessly, moving at an increasingly slower pace. Just when she thought she could walk no more; the smell of food caught her attention. She lifted her head high and sniffed enthusiastically. Driven on by hunger, she speeded up as she followed the direction of the irresistible aroma. When she reached the brow of a hill she looked around. In the far distance she saw a number of lights glimmering in the darkness. Then her attention was drawn to something much closer, just a short way from the bottom of the hill. It was a small fire. She could see that someone was sitting near it. It looked like there was a small building next to the person, but it was difficult to see exactly what it was. She could see the outline of a tree as well. Cici's nose led her down the hill towards the source of the smell.

It was not long before she found herself standing in the darkness but close enough to feel some of the comforting heat radiating from the fire. A man was on the other side of the fire. Exhausted, she sat down and stared at the man for a while as if in a trance. The little bit of warmth began to make her feel drowsy, but she had to keep alert. The man looked middle aged and had a short, black beard. He was sitting on a chair with a thick blanket wrapped tightly around him. There was a pile of cut twigs and branches next to him. The small building she could see from the hill was, in fact, a wooden caravan with wheels on it. Close by and almost hidden by the dangling branches of a tree was a very large, white horse. It was tethered to the tree by a long rope. Cici looked towards the fire. A cooking pot was suspended over it by a hook dangling from a tripod of poles. She knew she had found the food. She waited quietly and sat expectantly with her ears angled forward in eager anticipation.

The man looked on in silence as the thin, mud covered, weary animal emerged from the darkness. She looked so pitiful.

As Cici sat patiently by the fire, she desperately hoped the man would not chase her away. She felt so hungry. She was at his mercy as she had no energy left to run away. It was not long before he got up. Cici moved backwards slightly. He walked over to the front of the caravan, climbed up the wooden steps and disappeared inside the door. Several minutes later he came out holding a couple of bowls along with some cutlery and a bottle. He walked back to his chair and sat down. He placed a ladle inside the cooking pot and scooped some of the food out and poured it carefully into a bowl. He placed that bowl onto the ground beside him. Then he poured another ladleful of food into the other bowl. He waited a minute or so to allow the food to cool a little and started to eat from the second bowl. As he ate his food, he kept a watchful eye on Cici. When he had finished eating, he beckoned Cici. Obediently, she walked towards him and sat down in front of him. The man was surprised by her calmness and manners. He picked up the bowl of food from the ground and placed it in front of her. Despite her ravenous hunger, she lapped it up slowly as if savouring every bit of it. After she had finished, the man filled the now empty bowl with some water from the bottle, all of which she drank. Afterwards she moved closer to the man. He reached out his hand and stroked her as she bowed her head submissively. Together, they sat in silence by the fire.

Later on, the man wandered over to his caravan and went inside again. He came out with a large, empty sack. He shook it out vigorously, bent down and placed it beneath the caravan. Before he disappeared into the caravan for the rest of the night, he put a few more twigs and branches onto the fire.

Cici settled down a safe distance from the fire, benefitting from the warmth that it provided. Every now and again, she gazed at the sparks which floated effortlessly up from the fire until they no longer glowed in the darkness. She stayed there until the fire died down and she could no longer feel the heat. Then she crawled under the caravan and curled up tightly on the sack. As she lay there quietly, she heard the muffled sound of snoring coming from within the caravan above her. It was reassuring for her to know she was not alone in the darkness. It was not long before she drifted off into a deep sleep.

The new day came far too early for Cici. Creaking noises inside the caravan woke her. As she opened her eyes and looked around through the fine, dawn mist, she saw the man's horse standing by the tree, its tail swishing from side to side. Very close by, she saw a number of small creatures loping along the ground. They occasionally stopped to nibble the grass and then stood erect to sniff the air. They amused Cici so she watched them until they disappeared from sight. A little while later, the man emerged from the caravan. He was eating a hunk of bread as he walked towards the horse. He untied him from the tree and put his harness on, backed him up between the shafts and hitched him to the caravan. He hung a bag of feed over the horse's neck and then looked under the caravan. Seeing that Cici was still there, he smiled and then went inside the caravan returning with a bowl of scraps and some water for her. She was so thankful that she did not have to go looking for food. As she ate her breakfast, the man dismantled the tripod of poles and the cooking pot and packed all his belongings away inside the caravan.

When he was ready, the man climbed the steps onto the seating area at the front of the caravan and called to Cici to join him. There was no hesitation now as Cici bounded up the steps and sat next to him resting her shoulder against his leg as the horse began to trot off into the morning light.

As they travelled along the rough track, Cici felt the wind ruffling her fur. The man chatted to her about his life and adventures and only occasionally stopped to ask her the odd rhetorical question. Instinctively, Cici looked up at the man as if to engage with him and every now and then the man stroked her head in appreciation. It did not matter that she could not understand what he said to her but it felt good to know that she was safe and with company.

They continued their journey together at a slow and steady pace despite the ruts and potholes. It was not the most comfortable of rides as they bounced and were jostled from side to side and to and fro. Although they saw a few animals in the fields and hedgerows, they passed no people on the track. Later in the day, when they arrived on the outskirts of a small village, their journey ended. The man unharnessed the horse and tied him to a tree. It took him a long time but eventually he managed to get a small fire going and cooked some food. He fed the horse, Cici and himself before retiring inside the caravan for the night. This time he allowed Cici to sleep on the floor inside the caravan which she really appreciated as the weather had taken a turn for the worse.

The next morning, as the man opened the door, a gust of freezing wind slammed it back against the caravan with a tremendous crash. Cici jumped with fright and backed as far as she could under the furniture. The man laughed and tried to reassure her as he pulled the door closed with a bang. There was no way he could make a fire so he shared some hard bread and cheese with Cici. When he went out again, he hung onto the door with all his might to close it quietly. Powdery snow was whirling all around in the pale light of dawn. There had been quite a heavy fall in the night and the wind had blown the snow into deep drifts against the wheels and on the steps of the caravan. The man cleared the snow off the steps with his boots as he went down carefully to begin his morning chores. The horse's blanket was encrusted with little mounds of frozen snow on the side turned to the wind. He whinnied softly and stamped his hooves, puffs of frozen breath hung in the air. The man began to shovel vigorously to clear the wheels and shafts so they could get on their way again.

After a mile or so, he stopped and parked the caravan on a small piece of unused land very close to the village and tied the horse to a tree nearby. Then he set off on foot towards the village with Cici in tow. The first houses in the village were small and set back a little from the track behind wooden fences. Then there was a bigger house with a well in the front garden and a horse and cart at the side. He went up the path of this house, knocked on the door and waited patiently. The door opened. An elderly woman stood before him. She looked at him quizzically. The man, who was very polite and sincere, introduced himself and asked her if she had anything that needed to be repaired. She hesitated before answering and then remembered that she had a broken wooden chair. She closed the door and went and fetched it and the broken parts to show the man. He examined the chair. The woman asked him if he could help and what it would cost. He said he could fix it and quoted a reasonable price so she allowed him to take it away. It was a bit bulky and awkward to carry but he managed to get it back to his caravan. Cici followed behind.

As the man worked inside the caravan, Cici remained on the seating area outside, curled up tightly to keep warm. Her ears pricked up each time she heard a new sound – hammering and sawing. Once the man was satisfied with the job, he beckoned Cici as he headed back to the woman's house. She was very pleased with the standard of his work and paid him a little extra on top of the price agreed. Then they continued around the village, going from door to door but without success. Despite each rejection, he remained in good spirits as he jingled the coins in his pocket. He decided to call it a day and headed back to the caravan. Just then, Cici caught a whiff of something tasty so she doubled back up the side of one of the houses to a shed. The door was swinging to and fro in the wind. Cici waited for the right moment and dashed inside. She found a large, metal bin with a few scraps scattered at its base. She scoffed the scraps in an instant. Then she reared up on her hind legs and tried to shove the lid off with her nose and front paws but it was on too tightly to move. It was too heavy to push over. She would have to leave it and catch up with her friend. Suddenly, with a fierce howl, the wind rushed around the side of the shed. The door slammed and the catch fell into place. Cici was trapped. She scratched the door and pushed against it. She could no longer hear or smell the man.

When the man noticed that Cici had disappeared, he called and whistled and even retraced his steps but there was no sign of her. The wind was strong, and the snow was beginning to fall again. He had to get to the next village before it got dark. Progress was slow and he often turned to look back for Cici as he missed her company.

Back inside the shed, Cici found some old sacks and lay down with her head resting on her paws, watching the door. She felt hopeless. She thought about all the things that had happened to her since she had been abandoned by her master. She could not understand why each time she started to feel close to people and belong, it did not last. She longed to be safe, secure and loved. Eventually she fell asleep but woke with every creak of the shed and lay listening to the moaning of the wind. By morning, she was cold, hungry, and exhausted again.

Footsteps approached the shed, muffled by the thick layer of snow. The latch rattled. The door was dragged open, revealing the silhouette of a man holding a sack. Not waiting to find out his intentions, Cici bolted through the open door. Startled, the man dropped his sack and turned but all he could see were paw prints in the snow. He had only gone to put his rubbish out.

Instinctively, Cici headed to where the man had parked his caravan but when she got to the spot, the man, his horse and caravan were nowhere in sight. It was like they had never existed. She sniffed around the area for a while until she realised they were really gone. Feeling despondent, she walked back through the village and out into the wide expanse of snow-covered countryside beyond and continued on her journey in solitude.

Chapter Four
Then There Were Two

By early evening, she felt hungry and utterly exhausted. She longed to stop, rest and sleep. Fortunately, she stumbled upon a fallen tree. She walked along its length inspecting it and, as she did so, she found that it had a very large hollow in the base of its trunk. It was a good shelter from the harsh weather. A place she could rest in for a while. She went inside and curled up tightly. Soon she was engulfed in the oblivion of sleep.

Something was moving on her face, something warm and wet. There was a strong animal smell. Cici opened her eyes slowly. She blinked a few times against the light. It was a dog. He had thick, black, matted fur and a tatty left ear. He was lying on his front facing her, licking her face repeatedly. She tried to stand but it was too cramped, so she sat up. The dog sat up too. He was much bigger than her. They looked into each other's eyes for a few minutes. She noticed he had kind eyes. Then he stood up, walked outside, and waited. She followed. They walked slowly and the dog remained slightly ahead of her. Every so often, he turned around to make sure she was still close behind him. When she fell back too far, he waited patiently until she caught up with him. Occasionally, he walked by her side for a while and nuzzled into her neck as if trying to comfort her and to encourage her to go on.

The dog led Cici onto a path which descended a hill and began to follow a small stream. They

went down the low bank for a drink where the ice had thinned to small, broken patches caught along the reeds. There were animal footprints in the snow which zigzagged this way and that. Some were large and sunk deep while others were barely etched on the surface. The dogs could smell that birds had been there earlier but, although they sniffed about in the undergrowth, there was no sign of anything. In the distance, there was a lonely birdcall and then silence. Cici followed a set of footprints further along the bank until it became steeper and was overhung with trees and bushes. Whatever little creature had wandered there had vanished. There was a strong smell though and she began to paw at the ground, scuffing the snow and leaves away until some of the roots of the tree were exposed. As she dug furiously with both paws, earth flying behind her, her leg disappeared down a hole and threw her off balance. She jumped back with a yelp and then cautiously approached again. Below the hole she had made she could see a large cavity. First she stuck her nose into the hole, then her head. She growled softly. The space was not empty. Something big, brown and furry stirred, snuffling and sighing. Terrified of what she had disturbed, she turned around and ran back as fast as she could towards the dog which had been following a different scent upstream.

The weak, winter sun began to drop lower in the sky. It was getting colder too. Cici was feeling weary despite the excitement of her discovery and she began to hope that they would find somewhere soon to rest and eat.

They continued on their way until around a spur in the valley they saw a few scattered lights. As they approached the town they crossed some wasteland and a small car park towards a road, beside which was a wooden shack. At the front of the shack lots of different meats and loaves of bread were displayed on shelves. They could not believe their luck. They spotted the vendor snoozing on a stool at the far end of the shack. The dogs quietly sneaked behind the building. They waited a while and then, in one swift move, the dog whipped in through the door, reared up on his hind legs, and grabbed a chunky, lump of meat from the shelf without the man noticing him. Triumphantly, he returned to Cici with it gripped firmly between his teeth. They trotted off to hide behind a wall and shared the meat, savouring every mouthful. Cici was so glad her new friend was a good scavenger as she would not have been brave enough to steal anything even though she was so hungry.

Chapter Five
In the Town

The dog took the lead again and set off into the town at a brisk pace. It was now quite dark and the street lights reflected off the wet pavements and road in ribbons of yellowish light. The heaps of snow in the gutters were hard and dirty brown. The relative silence of the countryside was replaced by the swishing of busy traffic on the slushy roads, blasts of music or the sound of chatting and clattering plates as they passed shops and restaurants. The dog seemed to know where he was going as he weaved in and out of the people scurrying along the pavement laden down with their shopping.

Suddenly, the dog turned off the main road and up a cobbled street. It was much quieter and Cici felt relieved. It had been quite a while since she had been in a busy town and even then she had been on a lead. The street was lined with terraces and shops. There was quite a mixture of styles. Some new and tall, others short with sagging roofs and bulging walls. Old pan tiles, mossy slates and shiny roofs made a tapestry of shape and colour against the dusky glow of the town. Steps went up to front doors or down to basements. There were gates and railings, bins and boxes to negotiate. Bright, plate glass windows and small bays displayed a huge variety of merchandise. The dog, with Cici in tow, kept right on past all of these until he came to a shop which smelt wonderful. They stopped. Sausages! When a customer left the shop, the door was still ajar so the dog gently pushed his way in, but his luck had changed. Before he had taken many steps, the butcher leapt out from behind the counter, brandishing a broom and yelling. The dog bared his teeth and growled as he began to back away. The butcher kept coming though, shoving the broom at the dog until he was back out on the street again. Cici had taken cover behind a pile of rubbish when she heard the commotion. The door shut with a bang but the dog continued to stand there hopefully until the butcher disappeared from sight. They hung around the shop in case someone else went in or the butcher came out with a titbit for them but it was in vain. Eventually, the blind came down over the door and the light went out.

Several streets on, they came to a café at the end of a terrace. They walked around the side of the building until they reached an old gate into the yard. It was partially open and hanging off its rusty hinges. In the yard there were stacks of crates, plastic buckets, soggy cardboard boxes and bins. They both began sniffing around. Cici tried to get between a couple of stacks of crates, following a scent, when they wobbled and teetered and finally toppled over, bouncing and scattering all over the ground. Cici got quite a fright. She let out a little yelp and rushed back out of the gate and hid in the shadow of the building. The dog was momentarily scared by the crash but, being intent on getting to what he could smell, he pushed his way through the debris to a big dustbin. The lid was half off. Up he reared and hooked his front paws on the rim. He jumped back on his hind legs and with a clatter the bin was over and its contents spewed on the ground. He began to root through with his muzzle. Deciding that there was good stuff to eat he gave a short bark to encourage Cici to return. Cici hesitated for a bit and then crept over to sniff it. She licked at it cautiously at first and, having satisfied herself that it was okay, she started to eat and then the dog joined her.

Having filled their stomachs, the effects of the cold and wet, the darkness and their long walk began to take their toll. Cici saw some crates in a corner and circled around before lying down. The dog was restless. He paced to the gate and back, went to the gate and out around the side. Cici did not want to lose this friend so she wearily clambered out of the crate and followed. The dog was waiting at the corner. He was looking casually up and down the street. When Cici joined him, he sniffed her and then set off continuing up the road a little way.

A few doors up, there was a lingering smell of freshly baked bread, pastries and cakes. The bakery was closed but at the front there was a narrow, enclosed porch with a single step leading up to the entrance. Cici went in first. She paced about a bit trying to find the perfect spot and then lowered her body onto the cold, hard floor. The dog followed her in and lay as close as he could to her whilst facing the entrance to the porch. Cici felt the dog's heartbeat and the comforting warmth of his body as it nestled against hers. She felt safe in his company. Soon she fell into a deep sleep but the dog stayed awake and on guard.

As Cici slept on, the dog silently and vigilantly watched as people went past. Some rushed by without even noticing them while others glanced and walked on making tutting noises and muttering under their breath in an unfriendly way. A couple with children stopped and looked in making soothing noises but when one child started reaching his hand towards the dog, the adult pulled him back quickly and went on their way. The child looked back several times and then the group stopped. They were talking quietly. They retraced their steps. Then each child gently threw a small cake into the porch. The dog wagged his tail and snaffled the cakes down, licking his lips. The children laughed and then off they all went again. Feeling less threatened the dog started to relax and then, before he knew it, he drifted off to sleep as well. This was short lived. A young man was shouting angrily and punching the air as he walked menacingly towards them. His words were slurred and he was quite unsteady on his feet. The dog had learned that some people became like this at night but often wandered off without causing a problem. However, when this young man reached the step up to the porch, the dog stood up in a state of alertness just in case. He stood tall and brave. Cici cowered behind him for protection. The young man's face was contorted and ugly. He swung one leg at the dog. The dog crouched a little, getting himself ready but before the young man's foot could make contact the dog snarled, bared his sharp teeth, lunged sideways and caught the young man's ankle in a vicelike grip. He would protect Cici no matter what. The young man yelled out in pain and hopped about on his free leg trying to shake the dog off. The dog held fast until the young man lost his balance and fell to the ground writhing in agony and shouting for help. No one came. The two dogs slunk past the rocking form on the ground and headed off to find somewhere else to sleep.

Rather shaken, they continued through the ever quietening night in search of a safer place to sleep. Cici's paws were beginning to feel sore and she was relieved when they eventually stopped at a deserted bus shelter. They huddled together as far back as they could in one of the corners beneath a wooden, slatted bench. Sometime during the night, a scruffy, bearded man wearing a woolly hat and a crumpled overcoat walked in and sat on the bench above them. They remained as quiet and as still as they could and did their best not to be noticed. He shuffled about on the seat trying to get comfortable and, in doing so, his feet moved backwards under the bench. He felt his heels contact something solid and, curious to discover what it could be, rocked his upper body forwards with his hands gripping the edge of the bench and looked underneath. Much to his surprise, he saw two pairs of wide eyes staring back at him. He smiled kindly. Then he reached inside his coat pocket and pulled out a squashed chicken sandwich which was inside a clear, plastic bag. When the dogs got a whiff of the chicken, they were soon sitting bolt upright in front of him with their ears flopped forwards, eyes fixated on the sandwich with a steady, thin stream of saliva dripping from their mouths in eager anticipation. The man gently stroked their heads before offering them his sandwich. After a while, the man made himself comfortable on the bench and Cici and the dog returned to their corner beneath him. They all slept, without interruption, until morning.

They awoke to the sound of heavy traffic and the impatient tooting of car horns. The kind, scruffy man was nowhere to be seen. Just outside the bus shelter, they noticed that there was a young woman dressed in a long coat, gloves and headscarf. She was leaning forwards trying to see whether the bus in the distance was the one she wanted. Cici and the dog knew they needed to move on soon, otherwise there could be trouble for them when the other commuters arrived during the morning rush hour.

They sniffed enthusiastically, trying to detect scraps of food, no matter how small, as they wandered the streets. There wasn't much to be found though apart from a half-eaten packet of crisps and a couple of discarded pizza crusts on the ground near one of the cafes in the square. Cici got to the crisp packet first. She struggled to get the crisps out and, as she snuffled inside the packet, it got well and truly stuck around her white muzzle. She panicked as she felt like she was going to suffocate until she managed to free herself using her paws. Once free, she gripped the end of the bag between her teeth and shook it from side to side. The crisps scattered about her and she quickly hoovered them up, one by one. They were not enough to satisfy her hunger though. Cici turned around and saw that the dog had already eaten the pizza crusts and was licking his lips.

As they continued their search around the town, Cici noticed that there were lots of adult dogs and puppies on the streets. They were everywhere they went. Some were curled up asleep on the pavements, some were standing in the roads, some were lying inside cardboard boxes in the recesses and at the sides of buildings, some were standing around in packs or on their own on the streets and others seemed to be roaming around the streets, searching for something to eat, just like them. A lot of them looked scrawny and exhausted and some had visible injuries. A lot of them had a sad, pleading expression while others looked as though they were angry with the world. Cici also noticed that almost every time they came close to people on the street, most of them would scurry away. She could not understand why they seemed so afraid of her kind. It was an extremely rare occurrence that anyone would stop and feed or even stroke Cici and the dog.

Later that day, as Cici and the dog strolled along one of the streets together, they saw a lone dog standing outside a cafe ahead of them. He had large, pointy ears and looked as though he was staring down his nose, looking superior. Pointy Ears was taller than her but slightly smaller than the dog. As they headed towards him, he watched them intently. Cici felt uneasy. She was between the two dogs as they were about to pass. She tried to keep her attention focussed ahead of her and avoided looking at him. She quickened her pace in an attempt to pass him quickly. Just as she drew level with him though, without any provocation or warning, he lunged straight at her. Instinctively, she tried to dodge out of his way but he caught her by the scruff of her neck. She let out several piercing yelps. She struggled to get out of his grip. She twisted and turned, but he towered above her and had her flesh firmly between his teeth. Immediately the dog sprang into action. With hackles raised, eyes narrowed and a fearsome growl, his teeth were soon embedded in Pointy Ears' leg. He bit it as hard as he could. As Pointy Ears opened his mouth to cry out in pain, Cici seized her opportunity and made her escape. The dog did not release his grip until he was sure Pointy Ears was ready to surrender. When the dog did eventually let it go, with blood trickling down his leg, Pointy Ears limped away with his tail between his legs, whimpering in pain.

Cici was relieved when she saw Pointy Ears disappear into the distance. As she watched him go, the dog gently licked the small wound on her neck, cleaning and soothing her at the same time. She felt safe again.

The two dogs needed somewhere to rest and recover. They tried their luck down a cobbled alleyway. It was quiet here and there were gardens on both sides. Some had really solid gates to them, while others had wrought iron gates where it was possible to see right to the back of the house. They found a gate with a rotten bit at the bottom where they were able to crawl under into a small garden which contained numerous snow-covered mounds. There seemed to be a bit of a path winding between the mounds to the backdoor. The dog trotted along confidently and squeezed through the partially open door. Cici hesitated. It was strange to her and there was a damp and musty smell despite the cold. She did not like it. After a few moments, the dog's head appeared around the door. When he disappeared again, Cici followed cautiously.

Inside was a small dark room. The floor was strewn with bits of broken furniture and odd items that had once belonged to the people who had lived there. Pots and pans and broken plates lay scattered. Mould grew in some of them. The dog wasted no time here but turned through the door, along the hall and up the bare wooden stairs. They sniffed around the rooms here but there was little of interest. The old mattress on the floor in one room had seen better days. The wallpaper hung down in bedraggled strips. Plaster had fallen away in chunks from the ceiling. Cici and the dog returned downstairs. They entered the other room on the ground floor which was large with a big window. There was a worn carpet on the floor. Against the wall by the window, an old two-seater sofa squatted with one end propped up on books. A tatty, old blanket was draped partially over the back and onto the misshapen cushions. Satisfied that the place was empty and safe to be in, Cici jumped onto the sofa. She pawed at the blanket until she had created a nest for herself and then curled up inside it. The dog clambered up beside her with his back touching hers. He rested his head on the battered end of the sofa and finally they slept undisturbed for several hours.

They woke in the evening to the sound of dogs barking. The barking was getting closer and closer. Now wide awake, they sat bolt upright on the sofa waiting for the situation to unfold. Suddenly, there was a piteous yowl and a small, thin, black cat streaked through the door. It stopped in its tracks as soon as it saw Cici and the dog. It felt trapped between what was chasing it from behind and what was right in front of it. It looked terrified. Cici got down from the sofa calmly while the dog stayed where he was. She walked slowly towards the cat. It did not move an inch. Its breathing was rapid. It was as if it had resigned itself to its fate. When Cici reached it, she looked into its beautiful, emerald green eyes and then gently sniffed it. Sensing no threat from her, the cat responded by brushing the side of its face and body along the length of Cici's body. She could feel the pleasant rumbling of the cat's purr as it moved against her. It then walked over to the sofa and went underneath it.

A couple of minutes later the barking dogs, which had followed the cat's scent, had arrived at the garden gate. In their eagerness, they all tried to get through the gap at the bottom of the gate at the same time, which of course, they could not as it was far too small. The dog flew off the sofa and charged out of the house and into the back garden. He barked furiously and growled defensively as he tried to make himself sound as big and as fierce as he could to scare the intruders off. He was surprised when he found that there were not any dogs actually in the garden. Instead, he saw two heads and a leg poking through the gap at the bottom of the gate. The dogs were making so much noise with their squealing and yelping as they tried to push through. Seizing this opportunity, the dog waded in. First, he bit one of the dogs' muzzles. The owner yowled in pain and quickly scrambled backwards and disappeared. Next, the dog went for a right ear which tore a little as he pulled away sharply. Finally, he sunk his teeth into a leg before its owner managed to snatch it away. The sound of yelping receded and after some brief scuffling on the other side of the gate silence ensued. The brave dog crawled through the gap ready to face whatever greeted him on the other side but when he got there he saw nothing except for an overturned bin at the end of the alleyway. He waited outside the gate for a while just to make sure the dogs did not return and when he felt sure they had gone for good, he went back to Cici. As he entered the living room he saw that the black cat was sound asleep, snuggled next to her on the sofa. As gently and as carefully as he could, he climbed onto the sofa and curled up next to them both. They all slept soundly for the rest of the night.

Chapter Six
The Chase

Cici woke early the following morning. She saw the cat was still fast asleep next to her. She was curled up with her paw hooked over one of her ears. She looked so cute and yet so vulnerable. The dog was stretched out fast asleep snoring quietly. He looked very peaceful. Cici remained on the sofa content to watch over them and listen to the gentle sounds of their breathing.

Eventually the dog woke, stepped lightly off the sofa and trotted outside. The cat slept on. Cici yawned and stretched, nudging the cat. The cat opened one eye briefly and then resettled herself. Cici jumped down, sniffed the cat, stretched again, padded softly over the carpet and turned to take a last look at the cat before disappearing after the dog.

In the garden, the snow was beginning to melt and some of the strange shapes of yesterday were revealed - an old upturned wheelbarrow, part of a broken bicycle and a pile of old cushions, curtains and carpet. They began their daily search for food, sniffing around the backs of the houses. They found some scraps in the bins and in one garden where people had thrown food out for the birds. It was slim pickings. The dog led them back into town. The large, empty square enclosed by high, ornate buildings yielded nothing. The cafes were not yet open. They turned down a side street and came to the bus station. This was much busier. They checked in and around all the bus shelters. Cici found a crusty bit of bread on a bench. She turned her head sideways and caught it up with her tongue. It did not go very far to fill the hollow of her stomach. They continued along side streets until they found a huge bin. It was open. The dog leapt up onto a stack of pallets and then into the bin which was almost full.

He stood there amongst all the refuse. He could smell that there was something of interest down below so he pawed at the rubbish beneath him feeling sure that he would be rewarded for his efforts. Eventually, he found a juicy bone. He picked it up carefully between his teeth and jumped out of the bin. He took it over to the side of a house and started gnawing and licking it. Cici looked on, feeling very hungry and a little envious. After he had finished with it, Cici got her turn.

Soon they were on the move again, meandering up and down the busy streets dodging people and other dogs along their way. Above the general hubbub of the now busy streets, they could hear barking. They followed the sound until, as they rounded the corner, they could see a pack of mangy dogs further down the road, barking excitedly at something across the street. A large, black van crept along the kerb towards the pack of dogs. The sight of this van made the dog's blood run cold. He froze. Cici continued forward unaware. The dog's heart began to race with fear. He whined, pleading for Cici to come back to him. She turned around and sensed she was being warned of danger. They retreated together into a space between a wall and a signboard and cowered down silently watching. Two men, both dressed in black and wearing thick, protective gloves, got out of the van and went round to the back of it. They opened the back door. Inside, there were several large, empty, metal crates stacked on top of each other. They lifted two of the crates out and placed them, with their doors open, on the side of the pavement. Then they went back to the back of the van and pulled out a long pole each with a loop dangling from the end of it. The pack of dogs was still distracted and it was only when the poles appeared above their heads that they realised the danger they were in. Their mood changed. They became very agitated, snarling and growling at the men. A couple of the dogs lunged at the men trying to scare them away but when they tried to back off, their heads were caught in the loops. They thrashed around frantically but could not escape no matter how hard they tried. The other dogs scattered, abandoning the two caught dogs to their fate. The men then used nets with the poles to bring the dogs towards the open crates. The dogs pulled back, still trying to resist. It was a battle of strength but the men gradually got the dogs into the open crates and shut the doors firmly behind them. There was no escape for them now. The men then stacked the crates back into the van and shut the door, plunging the dogs inside into darkness. The men got back into the van and drove off. The sound of frantic barking could be heard as the van disappeared down the road.

Cici trembled for some time, even after the van had left. The dog sensed her fear and nuzzled up close to her trying to give her comfort. The dog had seen the black van around the town many times before. It never ceased to scare him. He had seen so many dogs being caught and imprisoned inside those crates. He wasn't sure what happened to them after they were taken away. He did not want to know. One thing he did know was that he never, ever saw those dogs on the streets again.

With great sadness, tinged with relief it was not them, Cici and the dog walked up a quiet side street towards a park. There were two teenage boys sitting on their bikes at the side of the entrance. They were laughing and joking with each other. Cici and the dog walked past them and went into the park. It was a beautiful, large, open space enclosed by a low wall. It had a wide path coursing through it, bordered by lots of trees. Grassy areas were emerging from under the snow. There was a large pond still partially covered by a thin layer of ice. People out for a brisk walk passed them. Children in the play area laughed as they were pushed on swings while others played chase around the bushes. A few ducks dabbled at the edge of the pond and crows cawed loudly from the tallest trees. A woman sitting on a bench threw some biscuits in the direction of Cici and the dog. They waited nervously until she walked away before approaching and sharing these titbits.

Suddenly, with whoops and shouts the boys on bikes rushed towards the two dogs. Ducks squawked and flapped across the pond and the crows rose in a cloud above the trees. The children were momentarily silent as they paused in their games. Cici and the dog leapt into action and pelted along the path with the boys in hot pursuit. The path forked. Cici bolted along one fork. Before she realised it, she had left the park, crossed the road, reached the top of a hill and found herself standing in the graveyard in the grounds of the town's church.

She stopped, panting heavily. She looked about her. She thought the dog had followed her but he was nowhere in sight. She felt very scared.

At the fork in the path the dog had hesitated briefly before leading the boys away from Cici. They chased him through the park and out onto the streets. The dog ran for all he was worth but the boys were gaining on him. He was getting tired. He had to lose them. He headed down a side street towards the main road. The boys began to brake using their feet, scraping along the ground to swerve to a stop just before reaching the busy crossing. The dog shot through the legs of the crowd, people scattering in all directions, dodged several cars and bolted through a gap in the fence of a building site. He leapt behind some bushes and lay panting. His heart thudded beneath his ribs. His lungs felt as if they would burst. He waited, trembling. Gradually, he calmed. No one came through the gap after him. He was safe.

Meanwhile, Cici had spent several long hours wandering around the town looking for the dog. It had been a very frightening day with dogs being captured and boys trying to run them over. It was starting to get dark. She was scared of being out in the town at night on her own with all the stray dogs and unpredictable people. She headed back to the old house by the cobbled alleyway. She managed to find her way there without too much difficulty and on the way snaffled a bowl of food scraps from behind a restaurant which were destined for the bin. When she got there, she squeezed herself under the wooden gate and went inside the house through the back door. She walked gingerly through the rubbish on the kitchen floor and went into the room where they had slept. She put her front paws up onto the sofa and peered inside the blanket. It was empty. She quickly went upstairs to check the other rooms. She paused at the top of the stairs. There was a quiet and rhythmic sound of breathing coming from the bedroom. She hesitated then crept in cautiously. There, on the end of the mattress, away from the window lay a cat. Cici moved forward more confidently and sniffed. Yes, it was the little, black cat. The cat woke with a start and fixed Cici with her big, emerald, green eyes. Recognising a friend, she stretched lazily, rolled over and went back to sleep. Cici was glad of the company and warmth of the little cat as she found a dry spot on the mattress, snuggled up next to her and listened to her purring. She stayed awake for as long as she could but eventually succumbed to sleep.

Back in the town centre, the dog had recovered sufficiently to ease himself to his feet and make his way back to the gap in the fence. He sat in the shadows looking out into the street. It was much quieter now. There was no sign of the boys on their bikes. The light from the streetlamp highlighted his head and then his body as he emerged slowly onto the pavement. He looked up and down the road and then set off at a walk and then a trot, retracing his steps. He picked up his own scent as he went back to the park. He tried the bins again and was in luck this time as he found a large piece of meat pie in a wrapper discarded there. His hunger satisfied, he continued along the path Cici had taken earlier. He picked up her scent here and there. Sometimes, where there were large puddles of melted snow he had to sniff all around to find the correct direction before he could set off again with any certainty. He left the park, crossed the road and walked up to the top of the hill into the graveyard. Behind a huge tombstone, the scent was quite strong. It must have been where Cici rested. The dog rested too and he dared to give a few short, hopeful barks. There was no reply, only another dog howling in the distance. The dog followed her scent around the edge of the graveyard and along a narrow alleyway. Cici seemed to have headed back down the hill to a busy street. Here the scents were too mixed up for him to follow and he encountered different groups of dogs. Some were quite territorial and the dog was exhausted and dejected. He slunk along trying not to draw attention to himself until he was back to a familiar cobbled alleyway.

In the small hours, Cici woke with a start. Something cold was pressing against her body. She stiffened with fear momentarily. She turned her head slowly. The dog was nudging her with his cold, wet nose. Soon, they were nuzzling and licking each other's faces. They were overjoyed to be reunited and in relative safety. The cat, disturbed by all this activity, took herself off on to the landing and sat cleaning her fur. The dogs gambled down the stairs with excitement watched by the unblinking eyes of the cat. At the bottom of the stairs they played, catching each other's legs and muzzles in their mouths as they rolled and wriggled with pleasure at being together again. They rested in between bouts but soon tiredness overcame them so they went into the big room, climbed onto the old sofa, curled around each other for warmth and drifted back to sleep. The cat padded silently down the stairs, across the carpet and crept close to Cici. She daintily curled her tail about her and closed her eyes.

After a good night's sleep the two dogs got up, stretched and yawned and sniffed around each other. The cat had disappeared. Cici checked upstairs but there was no trace. Their rumbling stomachs spurred them out into the cold morning and they cantered briskly down the alleyway, round the corner to the butcher's shop. They knew better than to try to sneak inside this time so they sat outside hopefully, eyeing up the lovely selection of meat through the large glass window. It was a popular shop and, as they waited patiently, they watched many customers come and go. One of the customers was an elderly woman carrying a shopping bag. She was wearing a long, thick coat with the collar turned up and a huge, furry hat. She paused briefly as she made her way to the shop and looked at Cici and the dog, smiling at them. She disappeared into the shop and returned a few minutes later with her shopping and a parcel in her hand. She approached Cici and the dog while talking to them in a friendly manner. The elderly woman opened the parcel to reveal two meaty bones. They were both desperate for food but each took their bone very gently from her hand before dashing back to the safety of the disused house and away from the attention of any passing stray dogs. Once they were indoors they set to with a will gnawing, licking and crunching for all they were worth. Cici lay on her front with her bone grasped between her paws as she licked and nibbled the marrow of the bone. Her rubbery, black nose bobbed up and down in a comical fashion as she tried to get further into the hollow of the bone with her tongue and front teeth. The dog was standing with one paw keeping his bone still as he ripped the meat away with his front teeth. Both dogs were fully focussed on their meal. It was the tastiest meal they had eaten in a while. As her hunger abated, Cici became aware of the cat who was eyeing the bones from her perch on the arm of the sofa. She must have crept in after a foraging trip. Cici had eaten most of the meat on the bone but there was still some left. She picked the bone up gently between her teeth and took it over to the sofa and placed it down just in front of the cat. Having sniffed at it delicately, the cat started biting little pieces of meat from the bone. She was so hungry. Cici curled up on the floor in front of the sofa while the dog continued eating his bone. It took time, but eventually, the cat had stripped all the remaining meat from the bone. She licked her paws and preened herself before curling up on the sofa to sleep. All three animals stayed in doors for the rest of the day comforted in the knowledge that they were safe together and well filled.

Chapter Seven
The Thief and The Old Man

The dogs awoke to a pale, wintery sun shining on them. The cat had not yet returned from her night's hunting. At the back door, the dogs stood side by side and sniffed the air. It was definitely warmer and a bit more of the snow had melted. The sunlight made the untouched snow sparkle and there was the sound of tinkling as melted water trickled down. It was time to set off again to find breakfast.

They returned along streets which were now familiar to Cici, towards the centre of town. The attitude of the people they passed seemed to be thawing too. Some even threw them the last bite of what they were eating and there were more scraps to be found. Even the groups of dogs they met seemed less aggressive.

The sun shone weakly on a small traffic island. There were a couple of dogs lying on the patchy gravel in the sun. Cici and the dog crossed the road and joined them. Although one dog got up to sniff them and the other raised its head to look, they were not warned off. Cici and the dog found a place to lie down together. They were content to watch the world go by and to nap when they wanted to.

By early afternoon the light was beginning to fade and it was getting colder so the dogs began to head home. As they set off down the street they heard angry shouting mingled with a distressed and frightened voice calling for help nearby. The sounds were coming from an alleyway and they went to investigate. From the entrance they could see a stocky youth pushing an old man. The old man did not fight back, instead he pleaded with the youth to leave him alone. His pleas fell on deaf ears and the youth continued to shove and punch the old man. The dog sensed the old man's fear and bounded towards the figures, barking a warning at the youth.

Cici followed at a distance, barking and growling. The old man fell to the ground as the youth viciously yanked something from his coat pocket and began to run off. He was not quick enough though and the dog launched himself at the retreating figure. His front paws hit him squarely in the back with all his weight and momentum behind them. The youth tripped and fell, sprawling on the ground. He scrambled to get up, trying to hit out at the dog which had him partially pinned to the ground. One mighty shove and a roll and the youth was up but the dog caught hold of his trouser leg and pulled with all his might.

The youth lashed out again at the dog delivering several hard blows to his head, but the dog hung on. The youth could not keep his balance and down he went again, landing hard on his backside. He levelled another punch at the dog, but he was not fast enough. The dog, in one swift move, let go of the trousers and caught the flying fist in his jaws. He clamped down. The youth squealed in pain. He dropped the stolen wallet in a bid to get the dog off his hand which was now bleeding and felt broken. The youth managed to kick the underside of the dog hard. The dog yelped and jumped back, releasing the fist but he continued to snarl and growl and moved menacingly towards the youth again. The dog was now between the wallet and the youth. The youth backed away clutching his injured hand. The dog stopped moving but his muscles were tensed and he was ready to spring again. His hackles were still raised and his teeth bared. The youth continued to back away and when he felt he had put enough distance between them, he fled down the alleyway and disappeared round a bend. The dog began to relax. He shook himself vigorously and turned to find the wallet. He picked it up carefully and carried it over to the old man.

The old man was sitting on the ground, leaning against the wall. He was holding his stomach with one hand and his head with the other. Cici was sitting, resting her body against his side and every now and then, nudged his arm or reached up to lick his face. The dog dropped the wallet in his lap, took several steps back and gave a single bark. The old man opened his eyes and took in the dog in front of him and noticed the warmth of Cici against him. He closed his eyes again and groaned. Slowly he put an arm around Cici and stroked her. The dog moved forward and flipped the wallet up with his nose. The old man looked down in disbelief – there was his wallet. He called softly to the dog and encouraged him closer. He stroked his head and chest while murmuring his thanks and praise. The three of them sat quietly for a while until the old man felt able to move. He used the dogs to help him get to his feet and steadied himself against the wall as he stood. He continued to stroke and pat them as he knew that if it wasn't for them, things could have been much worse.

The old man began to walk, weaving unsteadily and stopping at intervals to straighten up and catch his breath. The dogs watched him go but then Cici began to whine. He turned around painfully. Cici seemed to be pleading with her eyes as she wagged her tail. The dog hung his head and looked most forlorn. He knew he couldn't just walk away and leave them now. They had a bond. They needed him and he needed them. He whistled to them. Dutifully, they went to the old man. They walked either side of him, occasionally looking up at his face as he headed home. Along the way, the old man took his wallet from his pocket and popped into a small grocery store while the dogs sat and waited patiently for him outside. The old man came out with a couple of tins bulging in his coat pockets. The storekeeper came out too and stared at the dogs. He found it hard to believe the tale he had just been told, but seeing the dogs waiting patiently, he laughed and reached to stroke their heads. He then gave each of them a treat. Shaking his head and still laughing, the storekeeper went back in. The old man and the dogs continued along the road. At the next corner, he turned and stopped at the front door of his lodgings. He ushered them inside. He knew he was taking a great risk by inviting them in as he knew he was not allowed to have any animals stay in his home. Although it was wrong, he felt he owed it to them to give them a break from being on the streets.

The room was very compact. There was a single bed up against the wall on one side of the room, an armchair facing a small television and a coffee table. The dining area took up the other side of the room and contained a small stove, table and chairs and several cupboards. At the far end of the room were two doors. One door opened out to a small, sheltered yard and the other to a small bathroom.

The old man made himself a hot drink and then opened one of the tins he had bought and spooned some of the dog food into two small bowls. He set them down on the floor along with a bowl of water. The dogs ate the food and lapped up the water and when they had finished, they curled up quietly next to the man as he sat in his armchair watching a programme on the television. When the old man went to bed, the dogs stayed put. Soon they were all fast asleep. The only sound that could be heard was deep breathing and the occasional snoring.

The following day, feeling well rested and fed, the dogs needed to be let out. Most people in the building had gone to work and the old man had seen the landlady go off in a car with her friend. He decided to allow the dogs into the yard at the back. First he checked that the coast was clear and then he let them out one at a time. He cleaned up their mess with some newspaper and they settled down again together, nursing their bruises and recovering from the ordeal of the previous day. The old man knew he could not keep the dogs for long but he was enjoying their company. When the post came, Cici started to bark. The old man tried to grab her to quieten her. Cici was frightened and she cowered, creeping away to hide under the table. The old man felt terrible seeing that he had scared her, but he knew he had to keep her quiet. He talked soothingly to Cici but it was not until he had put down another bowl of food that she came out. The food was another worry for the old man as he could not afford to buy more.

During the second night of their stay, there was a commotion on the street corner. Two groups of dogs were fighting over territory. It was frightening. Cici and the dog began to scratch at the door and whine. They felt trapped and wanted to be able to run away. When things quietened down, the old man gave them the last of the food and let them out of the front door cautiously. He had to let them go but he would always remember them and tell everyone of how they had helped him. On the street again, Cici and the dog looked back several times before melting into the night. With a heavy heart, the old man closed his door.

Chapter Eight
Tragedy Strikes

The dog led Cici down many streets and alleyways in their continual search for food. They had entered a different and less familiar part of the town. It started to rain and the dogs felt quite miserable. They could not go back to the old man and they were now far from the disused house. They needed to find some shelter before the night turned colder. There were a few doors and porches here but the ones they found were already occupied. Eventually, they found some cardboard boxes which were fairly clean and dry as they were sheltered by the open lids of large bins. They made themselves as comfortable as they could but spent restless hours listening to the strange sounds and movements of this neighbourhood before deciding to go on their way again.

Since his encounter with the thief, the dog did not seem to be quite himself. He needed to stop and rest more and he often shook his head. Cici had to take more of the lead. It was hard as she did not really know where to go. Following her nose, she led them to a food stall in a layby. Drivers had pulled up in large trucks to get something to eat. Some of them had dogs in their cabs and did not mind Cici and the dog being around. Some even shared their burgers and buns but then the stall owner chased them off with his broom. They ran a little way and then the dog sat down in the dirt at the side of the road. Cici could tell all was not right with the dog. She sensed that if they could cross the road, they would find their way back to their well-known streets and the disused house.

As the dog looked on, Cici crossed the road. There was a lot of traffic on the road. She walked to the edge of the kerb and stopped. She waited patiently. There was a break in the stream of traffic. She seized her opportunity and rushed across the road. Safe on the other side, she turned and looked back at the dog. Now it was his turn. He waited. He saw his chance and began to cross the road, then for some reason he hesitated. The car bearing down on him braked and began to swerve but the dog turned and tried to go back to the side of the road. There was nothing the driver could do. There was a dull thud. Cici watched with horror as the car hit the dog, catapulting him into the air. He landed a few feet from where he had been. Cici ran back across the road. Horns blared at her and brakes squealed but luck was on her side and she made it safely to the side of her friend. He raised his head to look at her as she sat beside him, licking his face. He managed a little lick back on her nose, sighed and then slumped to the ground. Cici saw that the light had left his eyes but she tried to get him back by nudging him with her muzzle and gently pawing his chest. He did not move and looked for all the world as if he were asleep.

The truckers further up the road saw what happened and several of them rushed to the dogs. Cici growled protectively. One man squatted down, raised the dog's head and touched his chest. He knew the dog was dead and laid him gently back down. He reached to stroke Cici but she ducked and ran a short distance away, turned and began barking at the men. They returned to their trucks, shaking their heads in sorrow. This was not the first time they had seen an accident like this.

Cici returned to her friend and lay down beside him then paced up and down restlessly. She barked furiously and chased along beside any vehicle which came too close but always returned to his side. From time to time, a trucker walked down and tried to entice her away with a titbit but she was not interested in eating. She had lost her only real friend in the world. For the rest of the day and all night she maintained her vigil despite the cold and constant spray from passing traffic.

Chapter Nine
Captured

The following morning, a small van pulled into the layby and two women got out and slowly walked towards the two dogs. They spoke in low, reassuring voices. Cici backed off but did not bark even when one examined her friend. However, she would not let them touch her and she was not enticed by the treats they offered, even though she was cold, wet and hungry. For some time the women tried to reassure her and get close to her but Cici would have none of it. After a while, the women went back to their van and slowly drove towards the dogs and parked nearer to them. Cici began to bark as they brought a blanket out of the back of the van and placed it over the dog. They retreated to their van while Cici went back to her friend and sniffed at the blanket. She pulled part of it off the dog and lay down with her head on his chest. She was exhausted. When the women came back, Cici just wandered away with her head hanging low then she sat down and watched them as they wrapped her friend up in the blanket. Cici understood that these women were kind and not a threat to her, but she did not like them moving her friend. The women slowly began to carry the body of the dog to the back of their van. Cici followed. They laid the dog gently in a large, open crate and returned to the front of the van. Cici went to the back of the van and put her front paws up on the bumper and craned her neck to see her friend and to sniff him. She climbed into the van next to her friend. Gently, the wire gate of the crate was closed on her and then the door of the van. The van began to move. Cici was scared but she sensed that the women were trying to help her and she lay quietly beside her friend.

The motion of the van and the warmth of the heater soon lulled Cici to sleep. She opened her eyes every so often as the van bounced over a pot hole or swerved suddenly. The journey was not long and soon Cici was up and listening intently to the sounds outside the van. She could hear voices of people and lots of dogs. When the door opened, she blinked in the bright light and backed into a corner of the crate. She had no idea what this new situation would bring. The crate was opened gently. The women talked quietly to her as they lifted the dog out and laid him on the ground. When they walked away, Cici plucked up her courage and carefully let herself down from the van keeping low and crouching beside the body of her friend. She began to look around this small, fenced area. Beyond it she could see a whole, open compound with kennels along the sides. One of the women approached her and, as Cici was backed into a corner, she was able to slip a collar and lead over her head. A gate creaked open and she was led into the compound. The gate clanged shut. She was now one of a large number of dogs rescued from the streets.

The lead was removed but Cici did not try to move. Other dogs came up to her but she showed no interest. She sat with her head hanging low and then lay down with her head on her paws watching warily without moving her head. She was wiped out with the trauma of losing her friend. It was as if it did not matter what happened to her now. She was at an all-time low.

A short while later Cici crept into the corner of one of the kennels and dozed off. Something tugged at her tail. She pulled it away and resettled herself. Tug. Tug. It happened again and then something nipped her nose. There were a couple of black puppies trying to get her to play. She was not in the mood. She got up, circled around and lay down again with her back to them and her head and tail safely tucked away. Thud! Two paws pounced on her back and then began to scramble up and over her. With yips and yaps of excitement at this new game, the puppies would not leave her alone despite a few growls and yaps of her own. Cici was forced to get up and move. Once outside again, other dogs came over to sniff and greet her. Cici could not be bothered and just wanted to find somewhere to rest. Suddenly, there was a great commotion. Gates opened and closed with squeals and bangs and bowls of food were wheeled in on a huge metal trolley which clanged and rattled and squeaked at one wheel. The bowls were placed at intervals along the fence and all the dogs piled in with gusto. Cici wandered off in the other direction. She did not want to eat. She walked into another kennel and lay down. Light shone through a window behind the kennel. After a while, a door opened and one of the women who had brought her here came through it. She sat on a low stool near Cici and began to talk. Cici began to relax. The woman stretched out her hand towards Cici. She sniffed it and then let the woman stroke her back. She felt reassured that she would be okay, that someone cared and would look after her. Gradually, the woman brought out some titbits from her pocket and set them on the floor in front of Cici. She sniffed them and tentatively picked one up, then another and finally, following a short trail, she found herself eating a bowl of tasty and nourishing food. Maybe her troubles were over.

As Cici regained her strength and confidence, she found she even enjoyed rough and tumble with the puppies. Every day she met the kind woman who stroked her. Then one day, a lead was put on her again. At first, she resisted and began to pull away. She did not want to leave this place of comparative safety. The woman did not tug at the lead. She sat and talked to her and stroked her until Cici felt okay to go with her. They went to a white room with bright lights and a strong, sharp smell. There were other people there. They all sounded kind. One of them picked her up and put her on a table. Cici was a bit scared but the voices were calm and soothing. She felt a slight prick on her haunch. She was then given a treat and was taken to a large room with a couple of other dogs. Over the following days, she ate and rested and went out into a big field at the back where she could run and chase and sniff around to her heart's content. It was lovely, except for having to go into the white room for more injections and medicine every so often.

Chapter Ten
On the Move

One day, Cici and two other dogs were put into large crates. There was a blanket in each of them. It was okay because they were in a van like the one she had been in before. Then they were transferred into a bigger truck which was noisier and not quite so warm. They had food and drink and stopped to exercise along the way. The smells changed as the journey went on. At one point, there was a tangy, salty scent mixed with oil and fish. With bumps and jolts and clangs, the truck went up a steep ramp and onto a ferry. There was a constant low rumbling from the engine and the truck vibrated strangely. This was a new sensation. Cici trembled with fear. After lots of thuds and shouts, the engine noise increased and fresh air began to sweep over them. The truck slowly swayed up and down. It took Cici a while to get her balance so she could stand. Eventually she got used to the strange movements and was able to sleep.

The engine began to whine as the ferry shuddered and changed direction. Cici could hear the water churning. With thuds, clanks, shouts and squeals, the ferry stopped. What now? Cici was alert and a bit worried. The driver checked all was okay, started the truck and they were off again, leaving the smell of the sea and cries of seagulls behind. Cici relaxed and lay down to rest.

Finally, the brakes hissed, the engine was turned off and the back of the truck was opened. Cici was lifted out in her crate. There was a new voice and smells. A man put a lead on her. She was wary but he was kind and gently coaxed her out. It was good to be able to stretch and walk around after the restrictions of the crate even if it was only a car park. She was given food and water and then taken to a car. Cici did not want to get in at first as memories flooded her. Eventually, she was lifted in and secured in the back and the man drove off. The windows were open and Cici lifted her head and sniffed. She could see out and watched as the countryside flew by. The man chatted to her and his words sounded quite different to what she was used to but she was reassured as his tone was caring and soothing. They stopped several times on the way and each time Cici feared that she would be abandoned in this new and strange place.

Finally, they turned off the big road and began to travel through a town. Cici watched through the window as buildings flashed past. She caught the scent of water as they crossed a high bridge. The car twisted and turned through lanes, past homes and fields and then Cici could smell the sea again. Did this mean she was going on a ferry again? Was she to keep on travelling forever?

Chapter Eleven
A Place To Stay

The car stopped and Cici was taken through a gate into a garden. A friendly woman came to the door and out lumbered a huge but gentle dog. He was a bigger and better kept version of her old friend. His name was Will. They all went inside.

Cici was exhausted after her long journey. There were so many new smells, sounds and people to cope with. She retreated under the table and curled up in the corner to sleep. Will settled on a huge cushion by the fire. Cici just lay and watched until her eyes could stay open no longer.

Cici felt okay in her safe place under the table and Will occasionally joined her, sniffing and licking her in a really friendly way. When the door was opened, Cici followed him out into the garden. When he went to eat in the kitchen, she followed him and found that she had her own bowl of delicious food. The woman was kind and Cici began to pick up new words to 'sit' and 'come.' She also came to realize that her name had changed to Tilly which took a bit of getting used to and sometimes she would forget. Things were looking up for her and she began to feel hopeful that this could be a nice life. After a few days, Cici was put on a lead along with Will and they went for a walk. The smell of the sea grew stronger as they headed down a tiny lane. Then, there it was - a vast expanse of beach with the sea beyond.

Cici was so excited she jumped in the air, turned, and bucked on her lead which made the woman laugh. The lead came off and Cici ran and ran in ever decreasing circles until she was panting, and her tongue lolled out of her mouth and made her look quite comical. She then trotted after Will and began sniffing at the rocks and seaweed. Other dogs and their owners came up and some of the dogs played chase with Cici. She was **so** happy.

Back at the house, she began to relax too and even rested next to Will on the cushions but a knock at the door, new people or strange sounds sent her creeping back under the table.

Chapter Twelve
Home

One day, a new person came to the house. Cici hid under the table. This woman was jolly and seemed really excited and happy. The woman talked while she stroked Will's head, neck and back. Cici could see that it was safe and she liked the new person so she came out. What a fuss was being made of her! She was stroked and tickled. Toys were brought out for them to play together. Treats were offered. Cici kept really close to her, sitting by her legs and leaning her weight against her. When, at last, the woman got up to leave, she seemed a bit sad and so did Cici. She hoped to see her again. She could be a friend she could trust. She had a good feeling about her.

Some days later, the woman returned with a friend who was very quiet and calm. They stayed for a while and then Cici was put on her lead. She was happy to go off with these two. Maybe they would take her to run on the beach. Alas no. They wanted her to get into another car. Cici was torn. She liked them but her past experiences had taught her that getting into vehicles brought anxiety and change. It was frightening and she backed away pulling against them. She wanted to go back to the safety of the home she was staying in and to the huge, comforting dog.

They coaxed her gently, lifted her into the back seat and clipped her harness in. The windows were open but Cici was too apprehensive to do anything but be still on the back seat. The jolly woman turned around and stroked Cici as she chatted away trying to reassure her.

After a short drive, they stopped and she was brought to a new house. There were more new smells and different spaces. She trotted around, sniffing with interest. She found a water bowl and a food bowl. She found comfy cushions and sofas. There was a basket with a soft blanket by the warm radiator. From the patio door she could see a garden, fields, woods, and hills. Once she had explored every inch of the house and garden, she ate the food put out for her and chose a spot to lie down. Was she going to have to move again? The women sat and chatted quietly. Often one or other would move over to where Cici lay to stroke her. During the night, she curled up in the basket. All was quiet but she was unsure and restless, so she padded in and out of the rooms and she went to lie under the table in the kitchen for a while. One of the women came downstairs and curled up on the sofa near to Cici. Eventually, she relaxed and fell into a deep sleep.

After breakfast, Cici let them put on her harness and off they went for a walk. There were lots of other dogs and cats, judging by the smells. Down the hill they went to the stream. Each day, they explored different lanes and paths. Some of the things they encountered were strange but Cici's new friends showed her that they were not going to harm her. She returned to the house every day. Cici was truly loved by them and the trauma of her adventures began to recede in her memory. She was finally home.

About the Author

Nicola Hedges spent most of her life in London before moving to the South West nearly twenty years ago.

She has made some radical changes in career from civil servant to osteopath to teaching assistant. A period of ill health dictated yet another change of direction resulting in this, her first work of fiction. As the saying goes, 'When one door closes, another opens.'

Blue Poppy Publishing

If you enjoyed this book, we would love it if you could find time to write a quick review on our website www.bluepoppypublishing.co.uk .

Blue Poppy began in 2016 and has helped numerous authors, from Devon and beyond, to publish their books. We are still small, but we work very hard to ensure every book is well written and professionally produced. Some of our titles which may appeal to readers of *Cici: A Dog's Tale* include *A Clattering Beneath the Woods,* and *Teeny Tiny Witch,* we also have books for younger readers and for adults too.